Apples Here!

WRITTEN AND ILLUSTRATED BY WILL HUBBELL

Albert Whitman & Company ≈ Morton Grove, Illinois

X
7

MAIN

There are apples here,

hidden in buds and waiting for spring.

There are apples here,

scenting the air and waiting for bees.

There are apples here,

waiting for the sun and rain
to help them grow.

There are apples here,

waiting to be picked.

"Apples here!" calls the farmer.
"McIntosh, Gala, Golden Delicious
— all kinds of apples."

Apples for cider, apples for pies,

apples for applesauce on Hanukkah latkes,

apples to find in Christmas stockings,

apples to eat, and apples to share.

There are apples here.

Apples take a year to grow. Towards the end of summer, apple trees produce buds at the ends of their branches. These buds, which will become the next year's fruit, need the winter's cold to get them ready for spring. The warm weather of early spring brings **bud break**, when green leaves and flower buds burst out of their winter protection. Soon after bud break, flowers form on the trees. This is a very important time in the orchard, for all apples begin as flowers.

In the center of each apple blossom is a delicate part called a **pistil**. It is surrounded by other flower parts called **stamens**. Each stamen produces **pollen**, which looks like yellow powder. The pollen is carried from one flower to another by bees, which are attracted to the scent, color, and sweet nectar of the apple blossoms. When the pollen from one tree reaches the pistils on the flowers of another tree, seeds will develop and apples will form to protect and spread the seeds.

By mid-spring, the flowers that have been **pollinated** lose their petals and begin to swell into tiny green apples. Many of these will naturally fall off at a time called **June drop**. The apple grower also removes many of the little apples. This is called **thinning**. Thinning lets fewer apples grow, so they will be bigger. All summer, the fruit grows and ripens until it is ready to be picked by hand.

Stamen

Pistil

This part will become an apple

An apple blossom with the front petal removed

When an apple seed is planted, the tree that sprouts is unlike the tree it came from. Children are never exact copies of their parents, and this is true with apples, too. Instead of simply growing seeds, apple growers create trees by **grafting**, where a bud from one tree is combined with the young trunk and roots of another.

When fruit from an apple tree is especially good, the only way to make another tree just like it is by grafting. While only a few dozen apple varieties commonly end up in grocery stores, thousands of different kinds have been cultivated and named. There are varieties called Seek-No-Further, Brown Snout, Northern Spy, Winter Banana—there's even one called Esopus Spitzenburg! Apples are grown for different uses and come in many shades and combinations of green, yellow, and red; they can be firm or soft, sweet or tangy. Bitter apples have been used to make cider, and Rome, Crispin, and Ida Red varieties are excellent for baking and making sauce. Some apples are best just for eating: Golden Delicious and Gala apples are sweet and crisp; McIntosh apples have a hint of tartness.

Apple trees and people have been together for a very long time. The first apple trees grew wild in the mountains of Asia, and long before people wrote down history, the trees were spread to new homes by traders and farmers. The first books on apple growing were written by ancient Romans thousands of years ago. Apples traveled to the Americas with the colonists, and in the early years of this country, John Chapman moved westward with the settlers and helped spread the growing of apples. A generous man who led a simple life, he became famous as "Johnny Appleseed."

Over time, apples have become part of many of our traditions and holidays. They are fall gifts for teachers, and bobbing for apples is a favorite Halloween game. In the Jewish faith, apple slices are dipped in honey during the new year celebration of Rosh Hashanah, and applesauce is a favorite topping for the latkes made at Hanukkah. Once, apples were the only fresh fruit at Christmastime, and to this day, they are often placed in Christmas stockings. As healthy snacks, fresh apples are a common part of our everyday lives as well. It's hard to imagine fall without the pleasure of a fragrant and crisp new apple, one of nature's best gifts.

This book is dedicated to the Chelini, Datthyn, and Eaton families
and all the other growers that work year-round to bring apples to our table.

Library of Congress Cataloging-in-Publication Data
Hubbell, Will.
Apples here! / written and illustrated by Will Hubbell.
p. cm.
Summary:
Through the seasons, apples grow from buds to blossoms to fruit
and become part of people's lives and celebrations.
ISBN 0-8075-0397-5 (hardcover)
1. Apples — Juvenile literature. [1. Apples.] I. Title.
SB363 .H79 2002
634'.11 — dc21   2002000776

The illustrations are rendered in colored pencil with solvent wash effects.
The display typeface is Hornpype. The text typeface is Artcraft.
The design is by Will Hubbell, Scott Piehl, and Pamela Kende.